This Book Belongs to _____

Warner Press, Inc Anderson, IN 46018
© 2003 Warner Press, Inc
Printed in Canada

ISBN 1-59317-010-6

I Know I Am Special!

A Story about Ridicule and Self-Esteem

by Connie S. Owens   Illustrated by Jane Dippold

A true story dedicated to the special little boy who just wouldn't give up!
(And his very loyal sister)

Chris had what his mom called a "coloring book ministry." If anyone he knew was sick or sad he would just color a picture and mail it to him or her, hoping it would make that person feel better.

At bedtime he always included those people in his prayers, which became rather long sometimes as he asked God to bless everyone, including the dog.

A happy seven-year-old, Chris liked to ride bikes with his sister, Jenny, and to fish and play the piano just like his dad. He also enjoyed being on a softball team with his second-grade friends, even though it seemed like he always had to play way in the outfield.

Chris practiced softball in the backyard with his dad nearly every evening. He could hit the ball pretty well, and Mom and Jenny helped by playing catcher and outfielder—even the dog joined the fun.

Then one day at a game the pitcher accidentally hit Chris in the mouth with the ball. As his mouth started to bleed and swell, the surprised little boy began to cry.

The coach made fun of him in front of all
the other players, embarrassing him.

After that Chris was scared, and when he was up to bat, would jump back when the pitcher threw the ball. Instead of helping Chris, the coach kept making fun of him to the team players and to the other coaches.

Chris's mom and dad sat in the bleachers and
watched helplessly, feeling both sadness and anger
at what the little boy was enduring.

As the summer went by the problem got no better. One day when Chris jumped back from the pitched ball, the coach yelled at him, calling him a baby.

"That's mean!" cried Jenny as she watched
her brother walk slowly toward the dugout.

Unable to stand watching their son being hurt by the coach's badgering, Chris's parents told him he could quit the team. But the determined little boy would not give up.

Chris kept playing softball even though he was scared and the coach continued to yell at him. Finally, one of the other coaches began to work with him, helping the little boy overcome his fear.

Sadly, even after school started the teasing continued from some of the kids. Chris had some hard days and would often come home and sit on the steps with his arm around his dog. She listened as he told her his heartaches.

One day on the playground a bully yelled at Chris. "You are so stupid," he said, "You can't even hit a softball!" When Chris got off the bus that afternoon, he was in tears. Jenny followed sadly behind, not sure how to help him.

Cuddled up in Mom's arms with the dog and his sister close by, the little boy told her just how bad the teasing that was started by the coach, had gotten.
"I can't do anything right!" he wailed.

"Honey, you do lots of things right," Mom comforted. "I know their words hurt, but you have to know deep within your heart that you are special."

"But I don't play ball as well as some of the other boys," Chris said.

"Maybe not, but you send pictures to sick people, and you're on the honor roll and you can play the piano!" Jenny spoke up loyally.

"She's right," said Mom. "You know, honey, God had a plan for you when you were still a tiny baby growing inside my body. He didn't want you to be just like everyone else. He made you to be different and special."

"I am so sorry that you have been hurt by the teasing. Sometimes grown-ups, as well as children, say mean, unkind things. I am sure that both of you know other kids who are also teased unfairly."

"Yes," spoke up Jenny again, "kids on the bus make fun of Megan because she is a little chunky."

"And Will, because his skin is dark" added Chris. "Sometimes kids laugh at someone's clothes. Why are they so mean?" he wondered.

"I'm not sure," Mom said softly. "But now that you know how much teasing hurts, I hope the two of you will not make fun of others."

At supper that night they talked about it again. "In the Bible it says God makes each of us to be unique—special in our own way. No one else in the whole world is exactly like you or can do the many things you can do."

I know the plans I have for you, ... plans to give you hope and a future.

Jeremiah 29:11 (NIV)

That night when Chris said his prayers he asked Jesus
to let the other kids like him just the way he was.

Slowly, things got better. Chris even told a boy who was picking on him,
"You may play softball better than I do, but I can play the piano!"

Then one evening the little boy was listening to tapes in his room. Suddenly he marched into the kitchen and announced "I'm somebody! The words to this song say just what you did, Mom!" "I **am** important to God! I can do some things really well because that's how He made **ME**!"

"That's right," Mom said. "I know this has been a hard time for you, but you have learned how words can hurt. You have also learned that you are unique and wonderful. Why, **you are one-of-a-kind**—there is no one just like you!"

"Yes," said Chris with a very proud smile. "I **know** I am special because God made me that way!"

Dear parents,

Teasing and ridicule can cause even a happy, secure child to feel sad and to question his or her self-worth. Because self-esteem is often very fragile, it can be destroyed by the thoughtless, unkind comments of others.

As adults we must be conscious of modeling for our children an example of behavior that is accepting of others, despite differences.

A home setting where children are praised for their attributes and talents will provide them a feeling of confidence and security.

Parents and other caring adults can frequently remind children how special and unique they are to God, as well as to their families. Assure them—in the words of Mr. Rogers—"I like you just the way you are."

Helpful suggestions:

1. Prepare your children for life. You cannot protect them from all pain. They need to be aware that not everyone will be kind to them.

2. Share a painful memory from your own childhood when you were teased or rejected.

3. When your child has been hurt, comfort him by holding and cuddling him. Let her see your tears of empathy.

4. Help your child to ignore the offense and become a friend to someone who needs a special, caring person in his or her life.

5. Help your child turn from the rejection toward another talent or ability.

6. Frequently remind the child that God made each of us to be special and quite different from everyone else.

Connie S. Owens